Shumba's Big Adventure

There are lots of Early Reader stories
you might enjoy.

Look at the back of the book or,
for a complete list, visit
www.orionbooks.co.uk

Shumba's
Big Adventure

By Lauren St John

Illustrated by Lorna Hussey

Orion
Children's Books

First published in Great Britain in 2013
by Orion Children's Books
a division of the Orion Publishing Group Ltd
Orion House
5 Upper Saint Martin's Lane
London WC2H 9EA
An Hachette UK Company

1 3 5 7 9 10 8 6 4 2

The Orion Publishing Group's policy is to use papers that are natural,
renewable and recyclable products and made from wood grown in
sustainable forests. The logging and manufacturing processes are expected
to conform to the environmental regulations of the country of origin.

A catalogue record for this book is available from the British Library.

Printed and bound in China

www.orionbooks.co.uk

For Virginia McKenna, who, together with her son, Will Travers, and the Born Free Foundation, has devoted her life to saving lions and other precious animals and returning them to the wild

Contents

Chapter One

Shumba was the naughtiest lion cub in the whole of Africa.

When he was meant to be
getting his ears washed, he was
always off climbing trees.

And falling out of them…

When he was meant to be sleeping, he was chasing things that usually ended up chasing him.

When he was supposed to be
sitting with his mum, dad,
brothers and sisters, watching
the sun set, Shumba liked to
play games.

One night Shumba sneaked away to look for some fun. His mum had told him never to go near the road, so that, of course, is where he went.

First, he was nearly run over by
a truck.
Then a donkey cart only just
missed him.

Then something even worse
happened. A man with a big net
and scooped him up.

'Let me go!' cried Shumba.
'I want my mum.'

The man laughed. 'Here, drink this special water, little lion cub. And when you wake up you'll be in a new home.'

Shumba was so thirsty that he
drank the whole jug.

'But I don't want a new home,'
he said sleepily. 'I love my…
own…home.'

Then his eyes shut and he
began to snore.

Chapter Two

When Shumba woke up, he was alone in the dark. First, he thought his family had gone out hunting and forgotten him.

Then he remembered the man with the big net. He sat up and sniffed the air.

Shumba tried to walk but his
nose banged cold bars. He
peered through the bars.

'You're on a ship,' said the monkey in the cage next door. 'That's what humans call a floating house.'

'When can I go home?' asked
Shumba.
'You can't,' said the monkey.
'We are all prisoners, going to
the zoo.'

He waved a paw at the crates on
the deck. Shumba could see the
shapes of other animals. A tear
rolled down his face. He wanted
to be with his mum.

When morning came, a person
with a long mane like his dad,
unlocked his cage. She was
called Emma and she was kind.

'Poor little lion cub,' Emma said.
'You don't know what's
happening, do you?

Don't worry. I promise I'll find a
way to save you.'

She closed the door again.
'Right, one bowl of cat food
coming up.'

Shumba didn't want to eat it.

The ship kept rolling under his paws and making him feel sick.

For the next few weeks, things went from bad to worse. He couldn't stretch his legs, or play.

Instead, he had to listen to the sad cries of the other animals:

two gorillas,

parrots,

a zebra,

a python,

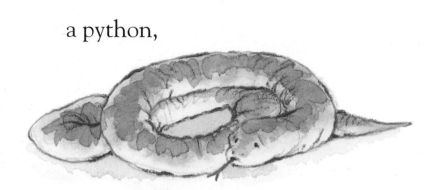

a dolphin,

two elephants

and some monkeys.

It grew colder. Emma brought Shumba a blanket but it didn't help. He longed to snuggle up to his mum's spotty belly.

One afternoon there was a big
crash. Shumba fell flat on his
face. The parrots squawked.

The sailors rushed around.
'We're sinking!' cried one.
But the ship wasn't sinking.
It was stuck on some rocks.

The sailors were so busy blaming each other that they didn't notice that the gorillas' crate was broken.

Before you could say bananas,
the gorillas were out on deck,
pounding their chests.

The sailors dived off the ship in fright.

Only Emma was not afraid. She unlocked all the cages.

'We're close to England,' she told the animals. 'If you make it, you'll be free.'

Shumba tried to be brave like his dad. He wanted to be free very much.

Chapter Three

Shumba jumped into the sea.
It was freezing!

The elephants made such a big splash it sounded as if a bomb had gone off.

Soon the water was full of
swimming animals. Shumba
found it hard to keep his head
above the waves. Luckily, the
kind dolphin gave him a ride to
the shore.

The animals set off to explore.
Soon they came to a noisy town.
Shumba didn't like all the
crowds, so he hid in a bush.

The others were having a
wonderful time. Through a shop
window Shumba saw the gorillas
chomping bananas.

The cheeky monkeys rode
around on trolleys and threw
eggs.

The zebra followed a woman
down the street.

She was wearing black and white stripes just like him.

The elephants went for a bath
in the swimming pool.

Five police cars raced down the street. They captured the gorillas and monkeys, and rounded up the elephants and zebra.

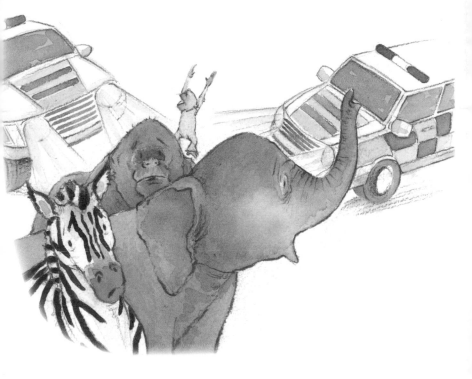

Shumba crawled into a garden.
A little girl found him. She took
him into her kitchen and fed
him bread and milk.

And a tin of tuna fish.

And a roast chicken.

And some scones and cream.

Shumba was so full that he was thinking of having a nap. Before he could lie down there was a terrible screech. It was the girl's mum.

'There's a man-eating lion in our kitchen!' she shrieked. Shumba tried to explain that he was quite nice really, but she called the police.

The little girl cried as Shumba was driven away. So did Shumba. His African home seemed a long way away.

Chapter Four

Shumba was moved to a zoo,
where it rained almost every day
and sometimes it snowed.

As Shumba shivered, people threw things at him and took photos.

One day, Emma came to see him. She had a plan to rescue the animals. 'You're going home,' she told Shumba.

She collected the elephants,
gorillas, monkeys, camel and
zebra and put them all on
a plane to Africa.

They dropped the gorillas in
the jungle and the camel in the
desert.

The monkeys swung from the trees in the African bush.

Shumba was the last to leave the plane. 'What if my family has forgotten about me?' he asked Emma, but she told him that mothers, like elephants, never forget.

It was true. When they reached
his home, Shumba's mum and
his brothers and sisters were
waiting.

'Where have you been?' asked his mum. 'I've searched high and low and far and wide for you. I've never stopped looking.'

Then Shumba's dad came home
and was very happy to see his
boy. Shumba had never had so
many cuddles and licks in his
life.

He told his family about the
ship, the kind dolphin, the
monkeys, and the zoo where he
was cold and lonely. He told
them about Emma who had set
him free.

Then the lion family moved to
a secret place where no humans
ever go and the only sound is
birdsong. When Shumba grew
up, he had a family of his own.
Every evening they would sit
together and watch the sun set.

His children loved to hear about
his adventures, but they all
agreed that there was no
place like home.

What are you going to read next?

More adventures with

Horrid Henry,

or go
exploring
with

Shumba,

and brave the Jungle

and Arctic

with Algy.

Find a frog prince with Tulsa

or even a big, yellow, whiskery

Lion in the Meadow!

Tuck into some

Blood and Guts and
Rats' Tail Pizza,

learn to dance with
Sophie,

travel back
in time with

Cudweed

and sail away in

Noah's Ark.

Enjoy all the Early Readers.